PUFFIN BOOKS

FAT LAWRENCE

Dick King-Smith served in the Grenadier Guards during the Second World War, and afterwards spent twenty years as a farmer in Gloucestershire, the county of his birth. Many of his stories are inspired by his farming experiences. Later he taught at a village primary school. His first book, *The Fox Busters*, was published in 1978. Since then he has written a great number of children's books, including *The Sheep-Pig* (winner of the *Guardian* Award and filmed as *Babe*), *Harry's Mad, Noah's Brother, The Hodgeheg, Martin's Mice, Ace, The Cuckoo Child* and *Harriet's Hare* (winner of the Children's Book Award in 1995). At the British Book Awards in 1991 he was voted Children's Author of the Year. He has three children, twelve grandchildren and two great-grandchildren, and lives in a seventeenth-century cottage only a crow's-flight from the house where he was born.

Dick King-Smith
Fat Lawrence

Illustrated by Mike Terry

PUFFIN BOOKS

PUFFIN BOOKS

Published by the Penguin Group
Penguin Books Ltd, 80 Strand, London WC2R 0RL, England
Penguin Group (USA) Inc., 375 Hudson Street, New York, New York 10014, USA
Penguin Group (Canada), 90 Eglinton Avenue East, Suite 700, Toronto, Ontario, Canada M4P 2Y3
(a division of Pearson Penguin Canada Inc.)
Penguin Ireland, 25 St Stephen's Green, Dublin 2, Ireland (a division of Penguin Books Ltd)
Penguin Group (Australia), 250 Camberwell Road, Camberwell, Victoria 3124, Australia
(a division of Pearson Australia Group Pty Ltd)
Penguin Books India Pvt Ltd, 11 Community Centre, Panchsheel Park, New Delhi – 110 017, India
Penguin Group (NZ), 67 Apollo Drive, Rosedale, North Shore 0632, New Zealand
(a division of Pearson New Zealand Ltd)
Penguin Books (South Africa) (Pty) Ltd, 24 Sturdee Avenue, Rosebank, Johannesburg 2196, South Africa

Penguin Books Ltd, Registered Offices: 80 Strand, London WC2R 0RL, England

puffinbooks.com

First published 2001
016 -16

This story was previously published in *Animal Stories* published by Viking 1997

Text copyright © Dick King-Smith, 1997
Illustrations copyright © Mike Terry, 2001
All rights reserved

The moral right of the author and illustrator has been asserted

Printed in Singapore by Star Standard

British Library Cataloguing in Publication Data
A CIP catalogue record for this book is available from the British Library

ISBN   978-0-141-31214-9

··· Chapter One ···

Cats come in roughly three sizes – skinny, middling or fat. There is a fourth size – very fat.

But seldom do you see such a one as Lawrence Higgins. Lawrence was a cat of a fifth size – very, very fat indeed.

He was black, and so big and heavy that his owner, Mrs Higgins of Rosevale, Forest Street, Morchester, could not lift him even an inch from the ground.

"Oh, Lawrence Higgins!" she would say (she had named the cat after her late husband, even though he had actually been quite small and thin).

"Oh, Lawrence Higgins! Why are you so fat? It isn't as though I overfeed you. You only get one meal a day."

And this was true. At around eight o'clock in the morning Lawrence would come into Rosevale through the cat flap, from wherever he'd been since the previous day, to receive his breakfast.

Then, when he had eaten the bowl of cat-meat that Mrs Higgins put before him, he would hoist his black bulk into an armchair and sleep till midday. Then out he would go again, where to Mrs Higgins never knew. She had become

used to the fact that her cat only ever
spent the mornings at Rosevale.

Five doors further down Forest Street,
at Hillview, Mr and Mrs Norman also
had a cat, a black cat, the fattest black
cat you ever saw.

"Oh, Lawrence Norman!" Mrs Norman would say (they knew his name was Lawrence, they'd read it on a disc attached to his collar, that day, months ago now, when he had suddenly

appeared on their window sill, mewing – at lunchtime, it was). "Oh, Lawrence Norman! Why are you so fat?"

'It isn't as though you overfeed him," said Mr Norman.

"No," said his wife. "He only gets one meal a day."

And this was true. At lunchtime Mrs Norman would hear Lawrence mewing and let him in and give him a bowl of cat-meat.

Then, when he had eaten it, he would heave his black bulk on to the sofa and sleep till teatime. Then off he would go again, the Normans never knew where. They'd become accustomed to the fact that their cat only spent the afternoon at Hillview.

··· Chapter Two ···

R ound the corner, in the next
street, Woodland Way, there lived
at Number 33 an old man called Mr
Mason, alone save for his enormously
fat black cat. It had slipped in through
his back door one day months ago –

at teatime it was – and he had read its
name on its collar.

"Oh, Lawrence Mason!" he would say
as, hearing that scratch on the back
door, he let the black cat in, and put
down a bowl of cat-meat. "Oh,
Lawrence Mason! Why are you so fat?

It isn't as if I overfeed you. I only give you this one meal a day and that's the truth."

When Lawrence Mason had emptied the bowl, he would stretch his black bulk out on the hearth rug and sleep till suppertime. Then out he would go again, where to old Mr Mason did not know. All he knew was that his cat only spent the evening at Number 33.

In front of Woodland Way was the
Park, and on the other side of the Park
the houses were larger and posher. In
one of them, The Gables, Pevensey

Place, lived Colonel and Mrs Barclay-Lloyd and their cat, who had arrived one evening at suppertime, months ago now, wearing a collar with his name on it.

Mrs Barclay-Lloyd had opened the front door of The Gables, and there, sitting at the top of the flight of steps that led up from the street, was this enormously fat black cat.

Each evening now at suppertime the
Barclay-Lloyds would
set before Lawrence
a dish of chicken
nuggets and a
saucer of Gold
Top milk.

"Lawrence Barclay-
Lloyd!" the Colonel would say. "I
cannot understand why you are so fat."

"To look at him," his wife would
say, "anyone would
think he was
getting four
meals a day
instead of
just the one
that we give
him."

When Lawrence had eaten his chicken and drunk his milk, he would hump his black bulk up the stairs, and clamber on to the foot of the Barclay-Lloyds' four-poster bed, and fall fast asleep.

The Colonel and his wife took to going to bed early too, knowing that at around seven o'clock next morning they would be woken by their cat mewing

loudly to be let out of The Gables. They never knew where he went, only that they would not see him again until the following evening.

··· Chapter Three ···

For a long while Lawrence was not only the fattest but also the happiest cat you can imagine. Assured of comfortable places to sleep and the certainty of four good square meals a day, he had not a care in the world.

But gradually, as time went on and he
grew, would you believe it, even fatter,
he began to feel that all this travelling –
from Rosevale to Hillview, from
Hillview to Number 33, from Number
33 to The Gables, and then back from

The Gables all the way to Rosevale –
was too much of a good thing. All that
walking, now that his black bulk was so
vast, was tiring. In addition, he suffered
from indigestion.

One summer evening while making his way from Woodland Way to Pevensey Place for supper, he stopped at the edge of a small boating-lake in the middle of the Park.

As he bent his head to lap, he caught sight of his reflection in the water.

"Lawrence, my boy," he said. "You are carrying too much weight. You'd better do something about it. But what?

I'll see what the boys say."

The "boys" were Lawrence's four
particular friends. Each lived near one
of his addresses.

Opposite Rosevale, on the other side
of Forest Street, Fernmount was the
home of a ginger tom called Bert, who
of course knew the black cat as

Lawrence Higgins. Next day after breakfast, Lawrence paid a call on him.

"Bert," he said. "D'you think I'm carrying too much weight?"

"If you carry much more, Higgins, old pal," said Bert, "you'll break your blooming back. Mrs Higgins must feed you well."

"She only gives me one meal a day," Lawrence said.

After lunch, he visited the second of the boys, who also lived in Forest Street, at Restholm, a couple of doors beyond Hillview. He was a tabby tom named Fred, who of course knew the black cat as Lawrence Norman.

"Fred," said Lawrence. "Tell me
straight, tom to tom. Would you call me
fat?"

"Norman, old chum," said Fred. "You
are as fat as a pig. The Normans must
shovel food into you."

"They only give me one meal a day,"
said Lawrence.

After tea he waddled round the corner into Woodland Way, where at Number 35 there lived a white tom called Percy. He of course knew the black cat as Lawrence Mason.

"Percy," said Lawrence. "Give me some advice . . ."

Percy, like many white cats, was rather deaf.

"Give you some of my mice?" he said. "Not likely, Mason, old mate, you don't need any extra food, anyone can see that. You eat too much already."

"Do you think I should go on a diet?' asked Lawrence.

"Do I think you're going to die of it?" said Percy. "Yes, probably. Old Mason must be stuffing food into you."

"He only gives me one meal a day," said Lawrence loudly.

Percy heard this.

"One meal a week, Mason," he said. "That's all you need."

··· Chapter Four ···

Later, Lawrence plodded across the
Park (being careful not to look at
his reflection in the boating-lake), and
in Pevensey Place he called in at The
Cedars, which was opposite The
Gables. Here lived the fourth of the

boys, a Blue Persian tom by the name
of Darius.

Darius was not only extremely
handsome, with his small wide-set ears
and his big round eyes and his snub
nose and his long flowing blue coat. He
was also much more intelligent than
Bert or Fred or Percy.

"What's up, Barclay-Lloyd, old boy?"
he said when he saw Lawrence. "You're
puffing and blowing like a grampus.
You're going to have to do something
about yourself, you know."

"The Colonel and his wife only feed me once a day," said Lawrence.

"I dare say," replied Darius. "But look here, Barclay-Lloyd, old boy, I wasn't born yesterday, you know. You're getting more than one meal a day, aren't you now?"

"Yes," said Lawrence.

"How many?"

"Four altogether."

"So at three other houses besides The Gables?"

"Yes."

"Bad show, Barclay-Lloyd," said Darius. "You'll have to cut down. If you don't, then in my opinion you're going to eat yourself to death. Just think how much better you'll feel if you lose some of that weight. You won't get so puffed, you'll be leaner and fitter, and your

girlfriend will find you much more attractive."

"I haven't got a girlfriend, Darius," said Lawrence sadly.

"And why is that, Barclay-Lloyd, old boy?" said Darius. "Ask yourself why."

"Because I'm too fat?"

"Undoubtedly."

"A figure of fun, would you say?"

"Afraid so."

"Actually, girls do tend to giggle at me."

"Not surprised."

Lawrence took a deep breath. "All right," he said. "I'll do it, Darius. I'll go on a diet."

"Good show, Barclay-Lloyd," said Darius.

"I'll cut down to three meals a day," said Lawrence.

"One."

"Two?"

"One," said Darius firmly. "One good meal a day is all any cat needs."

··· Chapter Five ···

For a little while Lawrence sat, thinking.

Then he said, "But if I'm only to have one meal a day, I only need to go to one house."

"What's wrong with The Gables?"

said Darius.

"Nothing," said
Lawrence. "They
give me chicken
nuggets and Gold
Top milk."

"What!" said
Darius. "Well, you
can cut the milk
out, for a start.
Water for you from
now on, old boy."

"But if I just stay
here," said
Lawrence, "the
other people will
be worried.
They'll wonder
where I've got to –

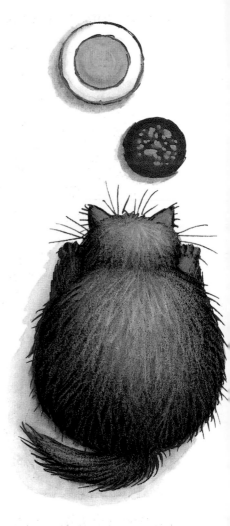

Mrs Higgins and the Normans and old
Mr Mason. And I shan't see the other
boys – Bert and Fred and Percy."

For a little while Darius sat, thinking.
Then he said, "There are two ways to
play this, Barclay-Lloyd. One is – you
continue to make the rounds of your
houses, but in each you only eat a
quarter of what they put before you.

Then that'll add up to one meal a day. Are you strong-minded enough to leave three-quarters of a bowlful at each meal?"

"No," said Lawrence.

"Then," said Darius, "the only thing to do is for you to spend the whole day at each house, in turn. And if you take my advice, you'll cut out breakfast, lunch and tea. Stick to supper. Which reminds me, it's time for mine. Cheerio, Barclay-Lloyd, old boy, and the best of luck with your diet."

··· Chapter Six ···

To the surprise of the Colonel and his wife, that Sunday evening Lawrence didn't touch his milk. He ate the chicken, certainly, greedily in fact, as though it was his last meal for some time, and he went to sleep on the foot

of the four-poster as usual. But the next
morning no mewing roused the
Barclay-Lloyds, and
when they did
wake, it was to
find Lawrence
still with them
and apparently in
no hurry to move.

On Monday, breakfast time came and went with no sign of Lawrence Higgins at Rosevale.

Lunchtime in Hillview passed without Lawrence Norman.

At Number 33 Lawrence Mason did not appear for tea. Old Mr Mason was worried about his black cat, as were the Normans. So was Mrs Higgins, but her worry ceased as Lawrence popped in through

the cat flap at Rosevale that evening.

"Lawrence Higgins!" she cried.
"Where *have* you been? You must be
starving."

Lawrence would have agreed, could he have understood her words, and he polished off the bowl of cat-meat that was put before him and hoisted his

black bulk into the armchair, and, much
to Mrs Higgins' surprise, spent the night
there.

On Tuesday evening Lawrence Norman appeared for supper at Hillview.

On Wednesday evening Lawrence Mason ate at Number 33.

Not until the Thursday evening did Lawrence Barclay-Lloyd reappear for supper at The Gables, much to the relief of the Colonel and his wife, who of course had not set eyes on their black cat since Monday.

··· Chapter Seven ···

Gradually everyone grew used to this strange new state of affairs – that their black cat now only turned up every four days.

And gradually, as the weeks passed, Lawrence grew thinner.

The boys noticed this (though only
one of them knew why).

"You on a diet, Higgins, old pal?"
asked Bert.

"Sort of," said Lawrence.

"You're looking a lot fitter, Norman,

old chum," said Fred.

"I feel it," said Lawrence.

To Percy he said, "I've lost some weight."

"What's that, Mason, old mate?" said Percy.

"I've lost some weight."

"Lost your plate?" said Percy.

"No, weight."

"Eh?"

"*Weight!*" shouted Lawrence.

"Why should I?" said Percy. "What am I meant to be waiting for?"

As for Darius, he was delighted that his plan for his friend was working so well.

After months of dieting, Lawrence
was positively slim.

"Jolly good show, Barclay-Lloyd, old
boy," purred the Persian. "The girls will
never be able to resist you."

"I don't know any."

"Well, between you and me and the

gatepost," said Darius, "there's a little
cracker living down at the other end of
Pevensey Place. Tortoiseshell-and-
white, she is. Dream of a figure.
Amazing orange eyes. You'd make a
grand pair."

Chapter Eight

So next morning Lawrence woke the Barclay-Lloyds early, left The Gables and made his way down Pevensey Place. I don't expect I shall like her, he thought, Darius was probably exaggerating. But when he

caught sight of her, lying in the
sunshine on her front lawn, his heart
leaped within his so much less bulky
body.

"Hullo," he said in a voice made gruff
by embarrassment.

"Hullo," she replied in a voice like
honey, and she opened wide her

amazing orange eyes.

"I haven't seen you around before,"
she said. "What's your name?"

"Lawrence," muttered Lawrence.

"I'm Bella," she said.

Bella, thought Lawrence. What a beautiful name! And what a beautiful cat! It's love at first sight! It's now or never!

"Bella," he said. "Could we be . . . friends?"

Bella stood up and stretched her
elegant tortoiseshell-and-white body.

"Friends, yes, I dare say," she replied.
"But nothing more."

"Oh," said
Lawrence. "You
don't fancy me?"

"Frankly, Lawrence, no," said Bella.
"I like the sound of you – you're nice,
I'm sure – but you're much too slender
for my taste, I've never cared for slim

boys. I go for really well-covered types.
As a matter of fact there's a black cat
further up Pevensey Place – I haven't
seen him about lately – but I really had
a crush on him. Talk about fat, he was
enormous! I do love a very, very fat cat,
and he was the fattest!"

She sighed.

"If only I could meet him again one day," she said.

You will! thought Lawrence. You will, and before very long too. And he padded away across the Park to be in time for breakfast at Rosevale,

followed by lunch at Hillview, tea at
Number 33, and then back for supper at
The Gables, including a saucer of Gold
Top and perhaps, if he could persuade
the Barclay-Lloyds, second helpings.
Oh, Bella, he thought as he hurried
along. You just wait!